THE HOLY GHOST IS MY FRIEND

Written by Catherine Christensen

Illustrated by Rebecca Sorge

CFI
An Imprint of Cedar Fort, Inc.
Springville, Utah

DO YOU KNOW WHO THE HOLY GHOST IS?

He's your friend, and He wants to
help you through your whole life.
This book teaches you how to know
when the Holy Ghost is with you,
the ways He can help you, and what
you can do to be constant friends.

ON EVERY PAGE, LOOK FOR A HIDDEN PICTURE!

To reveal the picture, all you have to do
is shine a flashlight behind the page or
hold the page up to the light. What will
you discover about the Holy Ghost?

The Holy Ghost can be with you anytime and anywhere because He does not have a physical body. After Jesus got baptized, something special happened. What did the Holy Ghost appear as?

The Holy Ghost came down
in the form of a dove.

A dove symbolizes peace.

Even though you won't see the Holy Ghost,
you can feel His peace.

On your birthday, you may get presents. After you are baptized, you also get a new, special gift unlike any other. At what age can you receive the gift of the Holy Ghost?

After you turn 8!

The gift of the Holy Ghost is the best present you will ever receive.

The Holy Ghost can comfort you, warn you, guide you, teach you, protect you, remind you, and help you in many other ways.

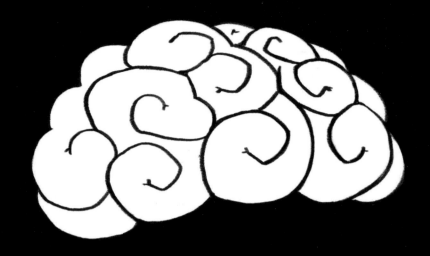

The Holy Ghost usually sends
us thoughts or feelings.

He may give you a warm feeling after you do
something good, or help you know what to say
when you share your testimony.

You can know your thoughts or feelings
are from the Holy Ghost if they encourage
you to do something good.

It's time for church and Cora can't find her shoes. Cora says a prayer so the Holy Ghost can help her remember where she left them.

Where could they be?

There they are!

The Holy Ghost can guide you
if you are quiet and listen to
the thoughts He sends you.

The Holy Ghost can guide you to know who needs your help and friendship.

Which children are happy or sad inside?

If you have a thought or
a feeling to do something
nice for someone,

that is probably the
Holy Ghost helping you
know who to serve.

Our lives are like this maze; you have many choices to make, and it can be hard to know if you're following the right path. Which way is the right way?

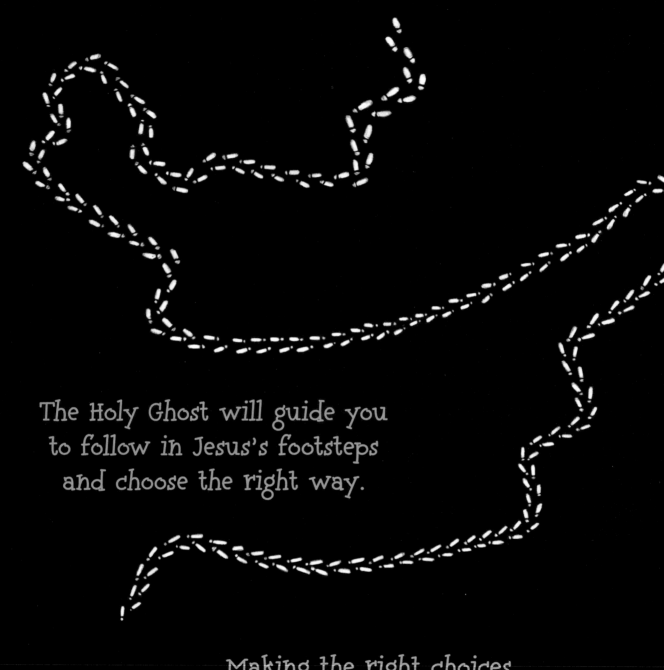

The Holy Ghost will guide you
to follow in Jesus's footsteps
and choose the right way.

Making the right choices
will help you be happy.

The Holy Ghost can act like a suit of armor to protect you from negative influences by giving you the strength to choose the right.

He can help you avoid inappropriate movies, books, websites, or music and pick better options instead.

Hannah thinks she should pay for the chocolate bar and say sorry. The Holy Ghost helps us know when we have done something wrong, and He can give us the courage to repent and make things right.

James has a feeling that
he should not cross the
road right now.

What is around the corner?

Oh no, a speeding car!

The Holy Ghost can warn you of physical or spiritual danger.

Sarah has moved to a new school and hasn't made any friends yet. How can the Holy Ghost help her feel better?

Sarah feels the comfort of
the Holy Ghost.

No matter what is making you
feel sad or worried,
the Holy Ghost can comfort you and
make you feel warm and safe,

like you are
wrapped up in a cozy blanket!

The Holy Ghost can prompt you to serve others—especially your own family. What acts of service can you see happening at home?

When you serve your family, you invite
the Holy Ghost into your home. He
brings feelings of peace and happiness.

7:14-25

How does the Holy Ghost help us when we read the scriptures?

What scripture story is on these pages?

One of the best ways we can invite the Holy Ghost to be with us is to read the scriptures.

The Holy Ghost can
help you understand
what you read and
know it is true.

The Nativity.

Reading your scriptures and
saying your prayers can help you
feel close to Heavenly Father.

The Holy Ghost testifies of truth, like the scriptures or testimonies. What is Sister Johnson bearing her testimony about?

Sister Johnson is testifying about Joseph Smith and the scriptures.

When you bear your testimony, the Holy Ghost tells other people that what you are saying is true. He also helps your testimony grow at the same time.

We can feel the Holy Ghost better
in some places than in others.
What holy place is behind these blossoms?

The temple!

The Holy Ghost can help you anywhere, but holy places, like the temple, the church, or your home, are the best places to feel the Holy Ghost.

Try to find quiet, peaceful places to pray and listen to the impressions the Holy Ghost sends.

If you try to choose the right and listen for
thoughts and feelings from the Holy Ghost,
He will always be with you, as your friend!

Jon, Juliette, and Calvin,
You light up my every day.
—Catherine

To my family.
—Rebecca

Text © 2017 Catherine Christensen
Illustrations © 2017 Rebecca Sorge
All rights reserved.

ISBN 13: 978-1-4621-2083-3

Published by CFI, an imprint of Cedar Fort, Inc.
2373 W. 700 S., Springville, UT 84663
Distributed by Cedar Fort, Inc., www.cedarfort.com

Library of Congress Control Number: 2017942205

Cover design and typesetting by Shawnda T. Craig and Kinsey Beckett
Cover design © 2017 Cedar Fort, Inc.
Edited by Chelsea Holdaway

Printed in the United States of America

10 9 8 7 6 5 4 3 2 1

Printed on acid-free paper